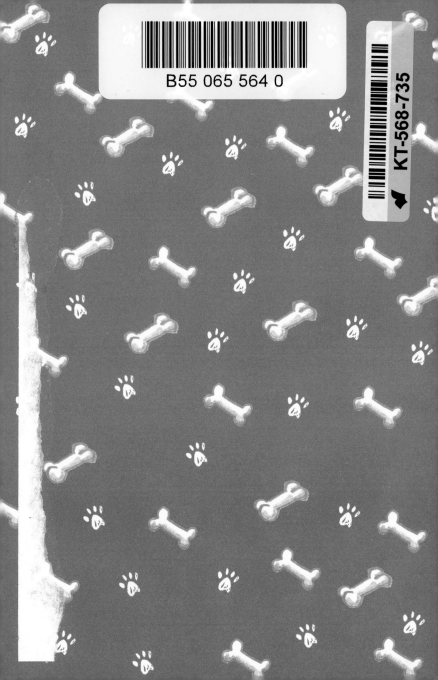

BONES
and
BISCUITS
LETTERS FROM A DOG NAMED BOBS

HODDER CHILDREN'S BOOKS

First published in Great Britain in 2020 by Hodder & Stoughton

3 5 7 9 10 8 6 4 2

Enid Blyton and Enid Blyton's signature are registered trade marks
of Hodder & Stoughton Limited
Text © 2020 Hodder & Stoughton Limited
Illustrations by Alice McKinley © 2020 Hodder & Stoughton Limited

A CIP catalogue record for this book is available from the British Library.

ISBN 978 1 444 95612 2

Printed and bound in Great Britain by Clays Ltd, Elcograf S.p.A

The paper and board used in this book are made from wood from responsible sources.

Hodder Children's Books
An imprint of
Hachette Children's Group
Part of Hodder & Stoughton
Carmelite House
50 Victoria Embankment
London EC4Y 0DZ

An Hachette UK Company
www.hachette.co.uk
www.hachettechildrens.co.uk

Enid Blyton

BONES AND BISCUITS

LETTERS FROM A DOG NAMED BOBS

Illustrations by ALICE McKINLEY

Hodder

Rogues' Gallery

BOBS

SANDY

PAT AND PITAPAT

THOMASINA

MISTRESS

GILLIAN   IMOGEN

Bobs and family live in Beaconsfield, Buckinghamshire. Their first house is called Old Thatch. It has a very pretty garden. They later moved to a house called Green Hedges, with an even bigger and more beautiful garden.

WUFF! MEET BOBS THE DOG . . .

Bobs was an inquisitive, cheeky and utterly lovable fox terrier who belonged to the author Enid Blyton. Bobs was part of a happy household that was full of animals, including other dogs, cats, tortoises, ducks and hens.

Enid Blyton wrote weekly letters to her young readers as if Bobs were writing them himself, telling children about the adventures he was having and the mischief he was getting himself into. The letters appeared in the weekly publication *Teachers World* from 1929 to 1945.

Blyton was devoted to Bobs, her very first pet, and continued to write the weekly letters long after the little dog had died of old age.

Dear Children,

Well, here I am with my book of letters for you! Tails and whiskers, when I look at all these letters I have written I'm surprised that my paw isn't worn out!

I am proud that I have so many friends. I am sure no dog is so lucky as I am. I have Gillian and Imogen to play with at home, and Sandy to sleep in my kennel to keep me company. And I have Pitapat to squabble with and Cosy, her kitten, to play with. There is old Thomasina in the garden to talk to, and there is Goldie the canary to sing me a song when I ask her. I wonder if you have as many pets as we have?

Paw-Shakes To
you all FROM
BOBS

Dear Children,

Yesterday we went for a walk with Mistress and Sandy was jumping about like a mad thing. Mistress laughed and said, 'Isn't Sandy full of beans this morning?' So I looked at him, and he did seem a little fatter than usual, though that might have been because of Christmas.

'Where did you find the beans?' I asked Sandy. 'You *are* a mean thing to gobble them up without offering me a single one! I shall go and find some too!'

So I went into the gardener's shed and poked about with my nose, which can smell much better than my eyes can see. And I found a box of nice red-coloured beans. So I ate them all up.

But bones and biscuits! I soon didn't want to run or jump about at all, like Sandy. I felt dreadfully ill, really I did. I went to Mistress with my tail down, and she said, 'Whatever is the matter, Bobs? Have you been naughty?'

2

And I said, 'No, Mistress. I'm full of beans.'

'Indeed you're not full of beans!' said Mistress. 'You look a very miserable little dog to me – not full of beans at all. I'd better give you some medicine.'

Then I asked Sandy if he had eaten a *different* sort of bean, to make him feel so frisky, but he said he hadn't eaten any beans at all. Well, boys and girls, I simply can't understand it. Can you?

PLENTY OF bEANS FROM BOBS

Dear Children,

Somebody grand is coming to visit Old Thatch. I don't know who it is. Mistress hasn't told me. It might be a king – or a princess! Fancy that! Do you know how I know? Well, Mistress has put a most beautiful white carpet down all over the garden at Old Thatch! I suppose she doesn't know quite which gate our great visitor is coming in – so she has laid the carpet all over the grass and the paths and the beds too. It looks and feels like white velvet.

I told Sandy not to tread on it with his dirty feet, but he said, 'How can I help it, silly? I must tread *somewhere*, mustn't I, and the carpet is everywhere!' So I'm afraid he has rather spoilt it.

Today, when the sun came out, I took a peep out of my kennel to see if our grand visitor had come – and, do you know, that beautiful carpet had got holes in it here and there! I don't know *what* Mistress will say! I am sure she

4

must have paid a great deal of money for it, and it is wearing very badly indeed.

I have asked Gillian to get a needle and white cotton out of her little work-basket and mend the holes, but she just laughed at me and said, 'Bobs, if you will get me a nice piece of warm ice to suck, *I'll* mend the snow carpet!'

Well, boys and girls, I've tried and tried to warm a piece of ice, and I simply can't. You might tell me how to; you are so clever, aren't you?

SNOW, SNiFFS aNd SNORTS FROM
BOBS

Dear Children,

Mistress was telling somebody the other day that dormice, hedgehogs and some other creatures hibernate for the winter. She said hibernate meant going to sleep in a sheltered corner, but first of all, she said, the animals had a very good meal and were fat and comfortable. Well, this sounded a splendid idea to me, because I often find it very cold in the winter. So I have decided to hibernate, too.

I have had a very good meal. I went into the kitchen and found the larder door open. I ate up all the fish that had been cooked for the cats. I ate three sausages that were sitting on a plate. I crunched up three bones out of the stock-pot, and bit a piece out of a jam sandwich. That was quite a good meal, wasn't it? I didn't think Mistress would mind, because, after all, if I hibernate she won't have to feed me at all in the winter, will she? So I shall save her a lot of money.

Now I feel fat and comfortable, just ready to hibernate for weeks and weeks. I am going to lie down and sleep on some old sacks in the potting-shed. If I don't wake up in time to write to you next week, I'll get Sandy to send you a note.

YOUR lOVING hibERNaTOR,
BOBS

Dear Children,

I can write to you this week after all. Gillian wouldn't let me hibernate! No, she came and looked for me in the shed, and when I wouldn't wake up she watered me with her watering-can. So I *had* to wake up.

I was cross. I said, 'How dare you wake me up out of my winter sleep? You don't go and wake up the toads or the tortoise or the hedgehog.'

'Well, you're *not* a toad or a tortoise or a hedgehog,' Gillian said. 'You're my dog and I want you to play with me. Come along!'

So I had to go. Isn't it a pity? I was just hibernating nicely.

Gillian wanted me to play at skipping with her. She has a new skipping-rope, but skipping is a difficult thing to do when you have four legs and a tail. I can make my legs skip all right, but my tail won't. It keeps getting in the way of

8

the rope. Isn't it a nuisance? Gillian says I'm stupid at skipping, but if *she* had to skip with four legs and a tail I think she'd be stupid too, don't you?

A SKIP OF MY TAIL FROM BOBS

Dear Children,

Whatever do you think! As if it isn't enough to have dogs and cats and canaries and goldfish, Mistress is now having things called catkins! I heard her talking about them yesterday. 'They do look so nice on the trees,' she said. 'I hope we have plenty of catkins.'

I pricked up my ears and thought to myself, *Bones and biscuits! If Mistress thinks I'm going to put up with catkins rushing about all over the place now, she is quite mistaken! Catkins, indeed! I suppose they are small cats. A mannikin is a small man, a lambkin is a small lamb – so it's plain to see what these catkins will be. Well, I won't be hissed at and spat at and scratched by catkins; yes, and I expect they'd come and gobble up my dinner, too, if I know anything about the cat family.*

So, boys and girls, I went hunting for those catkins. I barked up every tree. I growled fiercely in every part of the garden. I hunted everywhere for catkins; but they must have been rather scared, for, though I listened hard, I couldn't hear a single catkin mew, not one. And they all kept up the trees, too, for I didn't see a single one running about. So now I am happy again, for I really do believe I've scared those catkins out of their lives, and either they've run away or they're too frightened to show themselves. Ah, I'm a brave dog, I am!

A FEW TREMBLING CATKINS FROM BOBS

Dear Children,

Imogen sometimes does number puzzles with her mummy, and I listen to them. This is what they are – Mistress says, 'Suppose there are two cows walking in a field, Imogen, can you tell me how many legs you would see moving through the buttercups?' And then Imogen thinks and tells her the answer. But once Mistress asked her a puzzle, and she said Imogen's answer was right, and it wasn't. I'll tell it to you, and you'll see.

Mistress said, 'Imogen, suppose there was a cat sitting on the garden seat, and Bobs and Sandy ran up – how many animals would there be in the garden?' And Imogen said there would be three.

'Wuff!' I said, 'you're wrong!'

'No,' said Imogen, 'I'm right. Mummy says I'm right. She knows better than you do!'

So I called Sandy and told him, and he wuffed too, and

said, 'No, Imogen, you are wrong. The answer is *not* three.'

'Why isn't it three?' said Imogen. So we told her.

'Well,' I said, 'suppose there was a cat sitting on that seat and Sandy and I ran up – there certainly wouldn't be three animals in the garden – there would only be two – because the cat would have shot over the wall in a trice!'

What do *you* think the answer is, boys and girls? Pat says if the cat was herself, the answer would be ONE, not two – because she would fly at the dogs and they would be through the hedge before anyone could see a thing!

TWO dOgS aNd a CaT FROM BOBS

Dear Children,

Mistress has been telling you of the rhymes that Gillian makes up, hasn't she? Well – Sandy and I make up lots, too, and we wuff them in the garden, but nobody listens very much. They are very good, too. Here is one:

> *'When we go out we'd like to meet*
> *Biscuits walking down the street!*
> *Wuff-wuff-wuff!'*

Isn't that a sensible one? Here's another:

> *'Can you have a wag without a tail,*
> *Oh, can you have a wag without a tail?*
> *Does anybody know*
> *If a little wag can grow*
> *On a puppy-dog that hasn't got a tail?'*

We think that one's very good. We bark it loudly ever so often, and Mistress says, 'Whatever are those dogs making that noise for?'

I think my best rhyme is one that Gillian loves very much. This is how it goes:

> *'I've sniffed so many smells today*
> *That what do you suppose!*
> *I've got a dreadful headache in*
> *My whiskers and my nose!'*

Oh, boys and girls! You laughed so loudly over that that I do believe I heard you! *What* a noise! I think I'd better stop till next week!

A headache in my nose from BOBS

Dear Children,

Heyho, what a life for a dog! We've three more kittens. As if it wasn't bad enough having four puppies without getting kittens as well. I wonder Mistress doesn't start a Cat and Dog Home.

I've given up trying to count how many animals live at Green Hedges. As soon as I get the right number we get a few more kittens or something and then I have to add up all over again. Gillian says I'm not a very good adder.

'And I hope I'm not!' I said. 'I'm a dog, not an adder! I don't go sliding through the heather on no legs at all, putting a forked tongue in and out like an adder does!' That made Gillian laugh.

Gillian has been polishing her dolls' pram today. After she had finished it she polished up Thomasina's shell. Tails and whiskers, that tortoise does look new and shining! I asked Gillian if she couldn't shine *me* up a bit – so she tried.

Well, my fur coat won't take a polish at all, but, bones and biscuits, the tip of my black nose did! It polished up beautifully! I can see it shining every time I look down my nose at it – it is quite dazzling. It smells a bit funny though.

I'm longing for night to come because I know my nose will shine brightly then, and I mean to go out on the road and pretend to be a small bicycle with one lamp in front. I've been practising making a noise like a bicycle bell, and Mistress has just asked me if I've got a bad pain. Fancy her not knowing a bicycle bell when she hears one!

A TWINKLING NOSE FROM
BOBS

Dear Children,

I have such a funny feeling in my middle today, and so has Sandy. It's a good thing I don't write with my middle, or you wouldn't get a letter. Gillian says it must be something we have eaten. Well, we have only eaten nuts, and they are all right for eating, aren't they?

These were funny nuts. I will tell you about them, and you will know if they are not good to eat, because perhaps you have crunched some up yourself. You see, the gardener was cleaning the motor-mower, and had taken a lot of it to pieces. He had left all the bits on some paper, and had gone to get his dinner. Well, Sandy and I saw Pat sniffing at the paper and we ran up to see what she was smelling. We saw a lot of little grey things looking rather sticky and I said, 'What are those?'

Pat sniffed at them and said, 'The gardener says they are nuts. They belong to the motor-mower. They are oily.'

Well, I have often heard Mistress tell Gillian that nuts are good for her to eat because they have good oil in them. So I said to Sandy, 'Quick! Let's gobble them up before the gardener comes back.'

So we did – but, you know they didn't really taste nice, and were very hard to bite. And now, boys and girls, I rattle when I walk – and I'm dreadfully afraid the gardener will hear me and know where his nuts are!

A NUTTY RATTLE FROM BOBS

Dear Children,

I feel most uncomfortable. I've just been well washed and well brushed, two things that I think are really a waste of time. I would have run off and hidden myself, but Mistress tied me up before she got the bath. The worst of it was that she didn't bath Sandy too – she said he had kept himself nice and clean but that I looked as if I ought to belong to a sweep and go and sweep chimneys. So Sandy sat and laughed at me all the time I was in the bath. I glared at him, and got some soap in my eyes. Really, life is very hard some days.

I think I will go and ask a sweep if he will have me for his dog. How lovely it would be to be dirty all day long and no one to mind! No, I don't think I'll do that after all – I might fall down a chimney. I think I'll go and buy a nice new black coat, then Mistress won't know if I'm dirty or not. Don't you think that's a good idea?

Well, goodbye, children, I'm off to buy a black coat. Ho, what a shock for Mistress and Gillian when I come back!

SOME PATTERING FEET FROM BOBS

PS I didn't get as far as the shop after all. I fell into the stream and now I'm covered with black mud. Sandy says it's a cheap way of getting a new coat!

Dear Children,

I have a tame robin! Ah, you didn't know a dog could have a tame bird, did you? Well, I don't really know how my robin became tame, but it is really very fond of me. It even comes into my kennel! What do you think of that? It is a very tidy little bird and I think it comes to tidy up my kennel for me, because as soon as it hops inside it begins to collect all the hairs I have rubbed off on the straw. It picks them up with its beak and flies outside. Then back it comes to tidy up for me again.

I told Sandy I had tamed the robin, and he said it only came to finish up the crumbs of my dog biscuits in the dish outside. But when I made him lie down quietly in the kennel and watch, he saw the robin hopping *inside* too, and it soon began to tidy up again, picking off all the hairs it saw among the straw.

'There you are!' I said to Sandy. 'Haven't I tamed it? Do

you suppose there's another robin in the world that would come each day and tidy up a dog's kennel for him? Aha, I'm a wonderful dog, I am! I'm the only dog bird-tamer in the world! I wonder what it does with the hairs, don't you?'

I think I shall tame a hen next, and make it come and lay chocolate eggs in my kennel for Easter. Sandy says if a hen comes to live in our kennel he will go out. He says there isn't room for him and a pecking hen too; I do think he's selfish, don't you?

YOUR loVING biRd-TaMER,
BOBS

Dear Children,

Gillian came rushing indoors yesterday and when she saw me, she said, 'Oh, Bobs! There's a rabbit in the cabbages!'

Well, think of that! A cheeky rabbit, eating our cabbages! I couldn't have that, so out I ran to catch the rabbit.

I soon saw it, for its ears were sticking up out of the cabbages – but the funny thing was I couldn't *smell* it. I sniffed and sniffed, and thought to myself – well, this is the first time I've known a rabbit that didn't smell like one.

I crept closer and closer – it still sat there among the cabbages. I was shivering with excitement. I felt sure I was going to catch it – the first rabbit I've ever caught in my life. Then I jumped! I landed right on top of it, I caught it by the neck but, oh dear me, boys and girls, it was only a toy one! Gillian had put it there to play a trick on me.

You should have heard her laugh – just like a waterfall gone mad! I shall think of a trick to play on her now. Just wait!

TAILS AND WHISKERS FROM
BOBS

Dear Children,

Do you know, Mistress was so pleased the other day because the thrushes and the blackbirds were making a nest in our garden. I heard her say that they had eggs there that would hatch out into little new birds when they had been warmed and sat on.

She was so pleased about it that Sandy and I thought we would give her a nice surprise. So we thought we would build a nest! You see, we have plenty of good straw in our new doghouse to make one.

So we set to work. We made rather a mess in the yard, because the straw *would* fly out of the door whilst we were making the nest – but at last it was done. It is a beautiful nest with a nice round place in the middle, like a real bird's-nest. Sandy said it wasn't a proper nest unless we had some eggs in it – but the hens wouldn't give us any eggs, so we hunted about and found two old tennis balls, and we are taking it in turn to sit on them and keep them warm.

Won't Mistress be surprised to find two dear little ball-birds in our nest one day? I hope Sandy hasn't squashed them at all, because he does sit down so hard, and, you know, I have to keep my eye on him in case he forgets himself and *chews* our eggs!

JUST a few chews from
BOBS

Dear Children,

I was very frightened yesterday, because somebody began to move furniture about up in the sky.

Goodness, you should have heard the noise! I looked up into the big dark clouds, but I couldn't see anything there, yet that was where the noise was coming from.

I should think that quite a hundred wardrobes and about a thousand chests of drawers were rolled about the sky, and I was so frightened one would fall through the clouds and hit me that I ran indoors and hid under the bed.

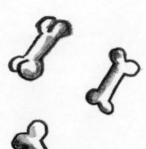

Mistress said it was a thunder-storm, but I know it was somebody doing their spring cleaning up there. Don't you think so?

Here is a tongue-twister that Sandy told me. Can you say it quickly? If a dog chews shoes, what shoes should he choose to chew?

A TWIST OF MY TONGUE FROM
BOBS

Dear children,

When Sandy and I were walking round the garden yesterday we saw a funny sight. The earth was heaving up in one little place, and we couldn't think why. So we stood still and watched.

'It's a little, tiny earthquake,' Sandy said.

'It's a huge, enormous worm coming up,' I said.

But it wasn't! What do you think it was? Guess!

It was Thomasina, the tortoise, waking out of her long sleep and unburying herself!

She has never slept so long before, but she said it had been so cold that she didn't feel like waking up. She has been there all the winter.

She shook out her four legs, opened her mouth to see if it would work, and then walked off to eat a lettuce.

She says unless the weather keeps nice and warm she'll

bury herself and go to sleep again. I hope it keeps warm, don't you, because it's nice to have Thomasina trotting about.

A few little trots from BOBS

Dear Children,

Gillian is growing mustard and cress, and dear me, isn't she proud of it, too! She goes to see her garden about a hundred times a day, and every time she sees it she calls me and Sandy and says, 'Look, you dogs – I believe my mustard has grown just a tiny bit since this morning! Oooh, won't it be lovely when Mummy lets me make sandwiches of brown bread and butter and my mustard and cress!'

'Did you hear that?' I said to Sandy. 'People can have *sandwiches* if they grow mustard and cress. Bones and biscuits! I wouldn't mind growing something, too, if I could have brown bread and butter to make sandwiches of what I grow.'

'Well, let's grow mustard and cress, too,' said Sandy. 'If we plant it like Gillian did, it will soon grow, and then we'll get Mistress to give us a brown loaf and a pound of butter to make sandwiches! Ooooh!'

Well, we found some mustard in a pot in the larder, but we couldn't find any cress. We didn't really know what it looked like.

'Perhaps pepper will do instead,' I said to Sandy. 'Yes – we'll plant mustard and pepper instead of mustard and cress!'

So we took the mustard pot and the pepper pot and we planted a spoonful of mustard and a shake of pepper. Then we put the pots back. And now we are waiting for our mustard and pepper to grow – it will be just as good as mustard and cress, I'm sure!

A PEPPERY SNEEZE FROM BOBS

Dear Children,

Do you like balls? Sandy and I love them. They are so nice and rolly, aren't they? We asked Mistress the other day if she would buy us some new ones because Sandy has chewed our two into bits and pieces and they won't roll any more. But she wouldn't because she said Sandy would only spoil them again. So we thought we must look about and find some ourselves. And we did! I'll tell you about it.

There is a funny game called tennis that Mistress plays sometimes in the garden. Well, she has six balls to play with – what a waste, isn't it? Why can't the players do with one? It would be quite enough. Sandy and I watched the people playing and we longed to have a ball too. When everyone went in to tea the balls were all left on the court, doing nothing. So I said to Sandy, 'Let's take them. We will leave them one to play with – that really is enough. We do need some new balls badly.'

So we took five of the balls and hid them in our kennel. When all the people came out after tea, what a hunt there was for those balls! Sandy and I didn't say anything. We just watched. And then – will you believe it? – Gillian came into our kennel as she sometimes does, and found all the balls! And Mistress gave her a penny for finding them – but we didn't get a penny for hiding them.

We aren't very happy.

A chewed-up ball from BOBS

Dear Children,

This morning six white ducks came swimming down our little stream from the next-door garden. They landed on the bank of our long pond and waddled into the kitchen garden. Mistress saw them there, eating our lettuces, and she called to me. 'Bobs! Bobs!' she said. 'The ducks are in the garden. Go and shoo them, there's a good dog. I'm too busy.'

Well, I thought, getting up, *I know Mistress is fond of birds and animals, and gives us dogs blankets if we are cold, but whatever does she want to give shoes to the ducks for? And fancy sending me to shoe them! Does she think I'm a blacksmith or a cobbler or what? Well, well, I'm an obedient dog – I'd better shoe them, I suppose!*

So I went into the nursery and hunted about for some of Imogen's old slippers. I thought Mistress's shoes would be too big. I found a pair of green bedroom slippers with rabbits stitched on the toes, and a pair of old galoshes. That

36

was all I could find. So I took them downstairs in my mouth and went to shoe the ducks. But they just wouldn't lift up their feet to be shoed! They quacked at me, and one of them pecked the tip of my nose. Then they all got into the water again and swam back home – without shoes. And, will you believe it, when Mistress came up the garden and found the slippers in the lettuces she was really cross with me!

'They're shoes for the ducks!' I said. 'You told me to shoe them!'

'I didn't mean *that* kind of shoeing!' said Mistress. 'I meant *this* kind – shoo, Bobs, shoo, shoo!' And she shooed me all round the garden!

Dear, dear, I wish people would say what they mean!

TWO SHOOS FROM BOBS

Dear Children,

This is the story of a bone. I found it down at the farm. It was a fine old bone, very smelly, and I carried it to Old Thatch. I left it in the middle of the grass and Mistress saw it and said, 'What a dirty old bone. I shouldn't like Bobs to have it!' She put it in the dustbin.

But I tipped the lid off with my nose and got it out. Mistress found it on the grass and said, 'Goodness! Here's that bone again!' And this time she put it in the coal-scuttle, meaning to burn it when there was a fire in the kitchen.

But I found it in the scuttle and quietly carried it off. I gnawed it on the grass, and forgot it again. And Mistress found it once more and was quite cross. 'Gracious me!' she said. 'Is this that awful bone again? However does it keep turning up?' So she took it and buried it in a corner.

But I dug it up and gnawed it on the grass again. And Mistress couldn't believe her eyes when she saw it lying there once more. 'That bone is bewitched!' she said. 'It keeps coming onto the grass, no matter what I do with it!' She took it and threw it on the rubbish-heap for the gardener to burn.

But I found it again and gnawed it on the grass. And this time, when Mistress found it, she wouldn't touch it. 'It's enchanted!' she said. 'Bobs, Bobs! Come and eat this old bone!'

So up I ran, and gnawed the bone again. And it is still on the grass, boys and girls, but Mistress has given up throwing it away!

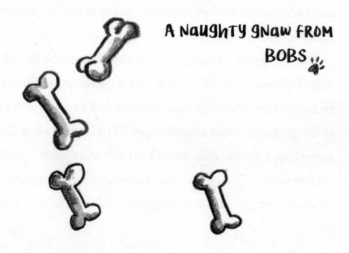

A NaughTY gNaw FROM BOBS

3rd June

Dear Children,

I have had another birthday, and I did have a lovely lot of cards and presents. I had a dog-brush, and seventeen balls and a sixpence, and I've forgotten how many dog biscuits (ooh, they were good!), and a new collar. I was so lucky!

Sandy is arranging to have two birthdays a year instead of one. But I say if he does he will get old far too quickly.

Do *you* think he will?

And I don't see how any one can arrange to have two birthdays a year, do you?

Sandy says he is going to buy them at a big London shop that says it sells anything in the world. Well, perhaps it sells birthdays, but I am sure they will cost a lot of money. Sandy is going to buy them tomorrow and bring them home in a paper bag. I've told him not to hold them too tightly in case they melt.

'If they do melt I shall lick them up!' I barked. 'Then I shall have had *three* birthdays instead of *one*!'

THREE OR FOUR LITTLE BIRTHDAYS FROM BOBS

Dear Children,

I've just had a bath. I wasn't dirty, and I didn't need a bath, so it was a waste of time. I hate having a bath – don't you? But perhaps you are like Gillian – she loves having baths, and she and Baby Imogen have one every day. What a waste of water!

Well, when I saw Mistress getting the tin bath ready out of doors, I thought to myself, *Oho! So that's what is going to happen, is it? Well,* I'm *going to hide the scrubbing-brush!*

So I ran up, took the brush into my mouth and hid it under a bush. But Mistress found it. Then I thought I would run off with the tin jug that Mistress uses to fill my bath. So I put it in the shed – but Gillian saw me and brought it back.

Then I thought of an even better idea – I would hide the SOAP! They couldn't wash me without soap, could they? No! So I ran up and got the big piece of yellow soap in my mouth. But I didn't have time to hide it, because Mistress came up just at that moment.

'Come on, Bobs!' she said. 'Here's the brush, and here's the . . . Oh, where *is* the soap?'

Well, I lay down and didn't say a word, because I had the soap in my mouth – and oh, boys and girls, it *did* taste horrid! Mistress hunted under the bushes and in the shed and on the tennis-court, but she couldn't find the soap.

And then Gillian gave me away. She shouted, 'Mummy, look! Bobs is blowing bubbles with his mouth!'

And so I was, because the soap was melting and every time I breathed, I blew a big bubble! *Wasn't* it a nuisance!

So I had my bath after all. I do feel nasty and clean.

A big bubble from Bobs

Dear Children,

Would you like to come for a walk with me? Come along then, down the lane and by the farm.

Wait a minute, wait a minute – don't go so fast. Can't you smell that really exciting smell just here in the hedge? Put your nose down to it as I do and sniff. That's the smell of a weasel! It is, really. It must have come here hunting for rats and mice last night. And just smell this little print here – that was made by a hedgehog. What, you can't smell it? Then there must be something the matter with your nose! Now, here's an easy smell. What animal has scampered along here? Come, come! You don't know? You can't smell anything? What is wrong with your nose? Why, that's the smell of rabbit, as plain as plain. Dear, dear, whatever do they teach you at school if you haven't even learnt the smell of rabbit! Why, any puppy knows that!

Sh! There's a freshly made track here. It smells quite

new. It's made by a rat. 'Gr-r-r-r-r!' Perhaps it's one that chases our chickens. Put your nose down and follow it. Come along. Here it goes, through the hedge, into the field – by the oak tree – and down that hole. Mister Rat lives there, does he? Well, I shall watch for him tonight! You can't mistake a rat smell, can you?

Could you smell it? What do you say – it smelt very sweet and fragrant? Good gracious! It certainly didn't! That was the honeysuckle you smelt, up in the hedge, not the rat.

Tails and whiskers! What a lot you have to learn, children!

ONE OF MY bEST SNiFFS FROM
BOBS

Dear Children,

Did you know that Gillian has a fine place to dig in, called a sand-pit? Well, Sandy and I went to look at it yesterday and we thought it would be grand to bury our bones there. So we did – but the next day, when she was playing in the sand, Gillian dug up all our bones and threw them away because she said they smelt boney and horrid.

'You shouldn't do that,' I said. 'They were *our* bones.'

'And this is *my* sand,' said Gillian. 'I don't like bones that smell boney.'

'Well, how would you like them to smell?' said Sandy. 'They can't help smelling like that. I like a smelly bone.'

'Well, I put them in the dustbin so they're smellier than ever now,' said Gillian.

So we went to get them, but, you know, they were right at the bottom, and we had to take out everything to find them – and when Mistress came along and found tins and paper and bottles all flying about the yard she *was* cross.

'Dear me, do I give you so little to eat that you must gobble dustbin rubbish?' she said.

'We want our old bones,' I said.

'They're too smelly,' said Mistress, and she gave us four new ones out of the stock-pot. Ooh! we *were* pleased.

We've buried them in *another* corner of the sand-pit this time, so we do hope Gillian won't find them!

A NICE SMELLY bONE FROM BOBS

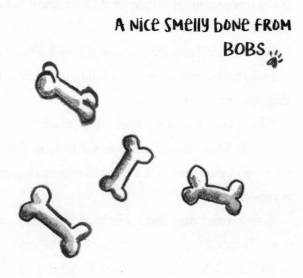

Dear Children,

I must tell you that something marvellous has happened.

Once, Sandy and I planted some crumbs hoping they would grow into biscuits and they didn't. Well, Sandy buried a bone the other day and when I was passing by the place this morning, whatever *do* you think it had grown into? Why, three fine kippers!

There they were, exactly over the spot where Sandy had buried the bone. Pat was there too, just going to eat the kippers, but I sent her off.

'They are what Sandy grew!' I growled.

Well, Sandy wasn't anywhere about, so I ate them in case they went bad. They were the best kippers I'd ever tasted.

Don't you think that's wonderful, to plant a bone and

make kippers come up ? I'm going to see if any more have grown.

YOURS TO a KiPPeR,
BOBS

PS I'm off to hide. Mistress has just called out, 'Who's stolen the breakfast kippers?' I didn't steal them, did I – but I ate them. And I thought they had grown, really I did.

Dear Children,

I am in trouble again, but it wasn't my fault, really.

You see, I went down to the river and I saw a lot of men there, sitting down watching a sort of rod thing which had a string tied at the end going down into the water. Sandy said they were fishing. I went and sniffed at all their baskets to see what they had for their dinners. One man had some delicious sandwiches, and somehow or other I found them in my mouth, though I really don't remember how they got there.

I felt pleased with the man for having such nice sandwiches, so I lay down by him and listened to what he was saying to the man next to him.

He said, 'I wish I could have a bite. I haven't had a bite for weeks. I *should* be pleased if I got a good bite.'

Well, wasn't that a funny thing to say, boys and girls ? I mean, people can't bear being bitten usually, and Mistress has always told me never to bite anyone – and here was a man longing for a good bite. I felt I really must give him what he wanted, as I had enjoyed his sandwiches so much. So I gave him a nice bite on his leg. But he wasn't a bit pleased. He jumped up. 'How dare you bite me?' he said.

I ran off with my tail down – but really, children, don't you think that man was silly to ask for a bite and then be cross because I gave him one?

A good fat bite from BOBS

Dear Children,

Mistress likes to tell us how to make a pot pourri. Well, let me tell you that I have smelt her pot pourri, and all it smelt of was old rose-petals.

Now, if it had smelt *really* exciting – of old fish and juicy bones, for instance – I could understand her making it. But why bother to keep a smell of roses? I never did care much for flower smells. Now Sandy and I are going to make a fine pot pourri of our own, which will be *much* better than Mistress's and have a really fine smell. Here is the recipe – please use it as much as you like . . .

Take three old bones from the rubbish-heap. Find the remains of a kipper and mix with the bones (but be careful someone doesn't eat it first; we had to go without because Sandy swallowed it by mistake). Add a few soaked biscuits, and sprinkle the whole thing with oil from a sardine tin.

Leave for a few days, and then open the jar when you want a fine perfume in your kennel.

Now, isn't that the best scent you ever heard of?

A FEW SNIFFS OF IT FROM
BOBS

PS The *best* thing about our pot pourri is that when you are tired of smelling it you can eat it all up!

Dear Children,

Will you please tell me something? How much would a seaside cost to buy? I'll tell you why I want one. It is because Mistress and Master and Gillian and Imogen all go off to the seaside in the summer of each year, and Sandy and I are left to guard Old Thatch. Now, if I could buy a seaside and put it in the garden, somewhere by the summerhouse, perhaps nobody would need to go away to find it, would they? So, if you know of any shop that sells seasides, send me a card and let me know. I have about sevenpence in my money-box, and surely that is enough to buy a really fine seaside!

Gillian says she is going to send me a jellyfish home. I do wonder what it will be like. Sandy says it will be a jelly made of fish, but I think it will be a fish made of jelly. Anyway, if it's the first, we shall eat it, and if it's the second, we shall put it into our bowl of drinking-water and keep it for a pet. We shall call it Shivery Shake, I think. Do you think it will learn its name and come when it is called? We would be so pleased.

Now everybody is starting off for the seaside, so I must go and wuff goodbye.

Ha! Wait till I buy my own little seaside! What a surprise for every one!

A Shivery Shake FROM
BOBS

Dear Children,

Three cheers and a loud hip-hip-hurray, they're back again from their holiday, all as brown as apple pips, hurrah, hurray, and three hip-hip-hips!

You'll know I'm glad, children, because I barked some poetry and I never do that unless I'm very happy and jolly. Then it just wuffs out of me.

Sandy and I, Binkle and Pitapat gave them all such a welcome. Pat has been moping, so she wasn't there. We didn't know where she was, so for the next three days we all of us hunted in the fields around to find her and tell her the news. Binkle found her, and when she heard the good news you should have seen how she hurried home!

The gardener has built Gillian a swing in the garden, and today Gillian told me she would give me a treat, so she lifted me on to the seat and then gave the seat a push. Oh, tails and whiskers! It went up and down, to and fro, and I kept slipping this way and that, trying not to fall off.

'You can go higher if you like, Bobs,' Gillian said and pushed the seat again. Up I went – and down I came, kerplunk, on the grass below! That's the last time I have a swing! Sandy laughed at me till he cried, but when I said, 'You go and have a treat too!' he wouldn't.

A few hip-hip-hips (but no haws) from BOBS

Dear Children,

I can hardly write to you. My tongue is hanging out of my mouth, and so is Sandy's. Both our tongues are so hot we can almost hear them sizzling. I'll tell you what happened.

Sandy came to me in great excitement this morning, because he said there was a little dish of custard in the gardener's shed that the gardener was going to eat with his sandwiches.

'How do you know it is custard?' I said.

'I heard the gardener say so,' Sandy wuffed.

'Let's go and have a lick,' I said. 'I feel like a nice bit of custard.'

So we waited till the gardener was out of the way and then we popped in at the shed door. We sniffed about and came to the gardener's sandwiches. We didn't dare to eat those because we have tried that before and we know what happens to dogs that eat other people's sandwiches. Well, we found a little dish by the sandwiches and we sniffed at it.

'That's the custard,' said Sandy, 'that yellow stuff inside.'

'It doesn't smell like it,' I said.

'Well, let's lick it and see,' Sandy said.

So we both took a good lick – and oh, tails and whiskers, that custard BURNT us! It did really! It sat on our tongues and burnt them like fire and we rushed out in a great fright. We put our tongues in water, but they still burn.

And when the gardener saw his dish had been licked, he said, 'Well, I never heard of dogs liking *mustard* before!'

So Sandy didn't hear right – it was mustard, not custard! I shall call for the fire-brigade to put my tongue out soon!

A VERY hOT TONGUE FROM
BOBS

Dear Children,

I had a real adventure yesterday. I went out for a walk with Mistress and she went to the station to buy a paper. Well, I went along behind her and I was thinking about biscuits and bones and not paying much attention to anything. A train came roaring into the station and stopped. I stood watching it, and suddenly I thought I saw Mistress getting into the train. I tore after her and jumped into the carriage just as the train was moving off – and bones and biscuits, boys and girls, when I looked up to see, it wasn't Mistress after all! It was somebody else dressed rather like her. And there was I, in the train going off to London Town, perhaps, and with Mistress left behind on the platform!

Oh dear, I really didn't know what to do. There were four people in the carriage and nobody took any notice of me. I expect they each thought I belonged to one of them.

The train raced on – and suddenly it stopped again at a

station. I jumped out of the window, because nobody opened the door, and fled to the station entrance, hoping that nobody would ask me for my ticket. I put my nose to the ground and tried to smell Home. I smelt what I thought was the right way and off I raced. And will you believe it, I got to Old Thatch just as Mistress did.

She was astonished. 'Why, Bobs!' she said, 'I thought I saw you getting into the train. What an astonishing dog you are!'

Wuff! I am, don't you think so?

A NICE TRAIN RIDE FROM BOBS

Dear Children,

A funny sort of wave has come to Old Thatch. I didn't see it come, but it's here.

Mistress says it's a heat-wave. I'm getting worried, because I'm sure I'm going to melt. I do wish I didn't need to wear a fur coat in the summertime. It's very hard on dogs to dress them like that, don't you think so? Why can't we dress in bathing-suits like boys and girls?

I told Sandy I thought I was going to melt, and he is sitting near me to see if I do. He says he will lick me up if I melt – but I don't think it's kind of him to say that, do you?

Oh, listen!

Can you hear the ice-cream man's bell? Mistress, please

buy me one, I do like them so much! They make my tongue so lovely and cold!

YOURS MElTINGlY,
BOBS

Dear Children,

We found a baby blackbird yesterday that couldn't fly. Gillian said we must put it in her canary's cage and the canary could look after it, but Mistress said that wouldn't do at all, because the canary eats quite different food from a blackbird. So I asked Mistress what blackbirds ate, and she said they ate worms and caterpillars.

But, you know, Mistress didn't give the little blackbird any worms or caterpillars, she fed it with little bits of bread and milk. So I thought *I* would feed it properly. Wasn't I kind?

So off I went and I soon found a big green caterpillar on a rosebush and a very long fat worm on the grass under the snowball bush.

I *was* pleased! I picked them both up in my mouth and trotted off to give them to the baby blackbird. But, oh, tails and whiskers, boys and girls, when I got to the cage, I hadn't got the worm and the caterpillar in my mouth! They had gone!

And where could they have gone? They must have wriggled down my throat, of course! I can't *bear* to think of a worm and a caterpillar having tea-parties together inside me.

A WORM and a CaTeRPillaR FROM BOBS

65

Dear Children,

Fancy – our dear little chicks have been stolen! Mistress wanted to know how it was that I didn't bark on the night they went, but, you know, I didn't hear a thing! So I think it must have been a rat (there is a big one that lives out in the field) or a slinky weasel or sly stoat. Have you seen a stoat or a weasel? They are very fierce little creatures, not a bit afraid of anything, not even me, so you can tell how brave they are!

Mistress has been reading some poems, so *I* am going to write one, too, to show you I can make up poetry nearly as well. It's a poem about our chicks, and Sandy and I bark it all the time we go wandering about the fields looking for the chicken robber. This is it:

> '*Someone,* someone*'s been playing tricks,*
> *And stolen away our dear little chicks.*
> *If it's a sharp-eyed, fierce little stoat,*

I hope he gets toothache all down his throat;
And if it's a horrible, savage rat,
I hope he meets an ENORMOUS cat;
And if it's a slinky, sly old weasel,
I hope he catches a nasty measle!'

There – that's our war-song as we go hunting for the chicken robbers.

Do you like it? Mistress says it is rather fierce, but, then, we *feel* fierce!

A STAMP aNd a YELL FROM
BOBS

Dear Children,

Bimbo is a funny cat. One day he is as round and as fat as a barrel, and his voice is big and deep when he meows. The next day he looks as thin as can be and his voice is little and squeaky. You might think he was a different cat. I asked him if he was always the same cat, and he said of course he was.

Mistress says it's because he's so very greedy. One day he ate my dinner and Sandy's dinner and Pat's dinner and his own dinner too, and he was too fat to lie down in his basket. Mistress says one day he'll turn into a nice, furry little pig and she'll build a cosy sty for him. I do hope he'll hurry up because I'd love to see him grunting in a sty.

Gillian fills the bird-bath each day now – and do you know what she does sometimes ? She waters Sandy to make him grow! He is very little, you know, like a puppy, so

Gillian thinks if she waters him he will grow big, like the flowers!

Isn't she funny?

A loving grunt from BOBS

Dear Children,

Mistress told somebody yesterday that a child had found a dandelion three feet long. So I thought I would go and find something wonderful too. But all the dandelions I saw had no feet at all. It was most disappointing.

Then Sandy and I saw a big spider, eight feet long! What do you think of that? We counted its feet and there were eight, there really were. So I told Mistress there was a spider in the garden eight feet long, but she laughed and said that we must mean eight long feet, not eight feet long. I don't see any difference at all, do you? I am four feet long, so is Sandy, so is Pat and so is Pitapat. But all the hens are only two feet long, and so are the sparrows. Isn't that right, boys and girls?

A clever dog came to see me the other day. He had found a pencil and he said he could draw.

'What can you draw?' I asked him.

'I can draw round oranges, balls and apples,' he said, and he looked as grand as can be.

'Pooh!' I said, 'I can draw something much more difficult than that. *I* can draw water.'

'I don't believe you,' said the dog. 'Show me,' and he gave me his pencil.

'I don't need a pencil,' I said, and I ran off to our big well. I sent the bucket down the well and made it come up full of water.

'There you are!' I said to the dog. 'Look at all the water I've drawn for you! Have a drink?'

You should have heard Sandy laugh! The roof nearly came off the kennel.

A bark four feet long from BOBS

Dear Children,

What a fright I got the other night! Buttons and buttercups! My nose shivers at the thought of it! I'll tell you all about it.

Sandy and I were sleeping quietly in our kennel, when suddenly we heard a dreadful thudding noise! Thud-bang, bang-thud! Just like that. We sprang up in our kennel, and growled. Then there came another bang, and another – right on our kennel roof.

'Burglars!' I said.

'Robbers!' Sandy said.

'Come to steal our biscuits!' I growled.

'Come to get my best bone!' Sandy wuffed.

'Let's go and bite them!' I cried, so out we rushed, as brave as could be. But will you believe it, those robbers weren't a bit frightened. No, they just sat up in the tree over our kennel and threw things at us!

'Bang!' Something hard hit me on the nose.

'Thud!' Something hit Sandy on the tail, and he yelped and fled into the kennel at once. But I stayed outside, barking. Then something hit me on the back, and two things struck my head – so I thought I would be safer inside the kennel. I didn't want to be killed.

In the morning, boys and girls, we looked for the robbers, but there weren't any. It was the wind that had blown all the apples off the tree, and they had come thudding into our yard! I did feel silly!

A bang-Thud fROM
BOBS

Dear Children,

Last night in the garden there grew up a most enormous white thing. I asked Gillian what it was, and she said it was a toadstool.

Fancy that! Did you know that toads grew stools for themselves? Well, I told Sandy and he said it would be fun to see which toad it belonged to, so we went and sat by it to see which toad in the garden came to sit on it. But though we waited for ages, no toad came. So we thought we would go and get one.

Well, I found one first, crawling along in the wet grass. So I picked it up in my mouth – quite gently, you know – to take it to sit on the toadstool. But oh, bones and biscuits! Boys and girls, it suddenly made itself taste so horrible that I simply had to drop it! I hung my tongue out and then rushed off for a drink of water. Sandy laughed at me and wuffed, 'Is the toad too heavy? Poor old Bobs!'

So I said, 'Well, see if you can carry it, Sandy. You may be stronger than I am!'

'Of course I am,' said Sandy, so he picked up the toad at once and ran to the toadstool with it. And then, boys and girls, a dreadful expression came over bis face, and he dropped the toad in a hurry! He had tasted it too! So he went to have a drink as well.

Then he said, 'Well, if no toad sits on that stool, I'm not going to waste it. I'll sit on it myself.'

So he did – and now there isn't much of that lovely big toadstool left!

A NiCE biT OF TOAdSTOOI FROM BOBS

Dear Children,

The other day I was very worried. I kept hearing a funny sort of rustling noise wherever I went. I told Sandy about it, and he said *he* couldn't hear anything! I looked all round to see what could be making the noise, and I saw a little wagtail bird sitting on the top of our kennel, wagging her tail up and down. 'Your tail wants oiling!' I said. 'I can hear it making a funny noise!'

The wagtail said, 'Chissic! Chissic!' and flew away in a temper.

Well, it couldn't have been her tail after all, because I could still hear the noise after she had gone. So I looked round again and saw Binkle coming to have a taste of our biscuits. And I thought *he* must be making the funny noise, and I said, 'Binkle, your legs want oiling!'

'And yours want boiling!' Binkle said rudely. He can be very cheeky, and the worst of it is I can never think of anything cheeky to say back to him before he runs off!

Well, it wasn't Binkle's legs, because I could *still* hear that noise when he was gone. Then I looked at Sandy and his tail was wagging, so I thought the noise must come from that.

And I said, 'Sandy, your tail must have got rusty. I can hear it make a noise as it wags.'

Then Sandy got up and looked at me closely, and he said, 'Bobs, you have a dead leaf stuck in your collar! Every time you move, it rustles – and you think you can hear someone making noises!'

Well, it *was* the leaf! When I took it out of my collar, all the noises stopped! Sandy says my brains want oiling!

A Tight Collar from Bobs

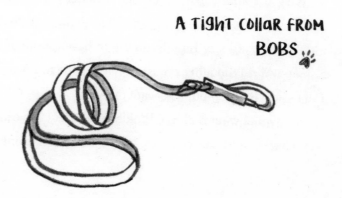

Dear Children,

Do you like onions? I don't. They smell so funny. The gardener has been digging them all up out of the garden, and he told Gillian she should have some in her soup. I saw him taking a basketful to the kitchen and giving them to the cook.

This morning I saw the gardener with his barrow full of something, so I went to see what was in it. There were heaps of onions there, but they didn't smell so horrid as onions usually do. When the gardener went to his dinner I thought I would really be a helpful dog for once, and take some of the onions to the kitchen for Cook. Then perhaps she would give me a bone or a biscuit. So I took a mouthful of the onions and trotted off to the kitchen. Cook wasn't there, so I put them on the mat. Then off I went again and fetched another mouthful of onions and another and another. I really did work hard.

Then, tails and whiskers! I heard Cook calling out of her window to the gardener, 'What have you brought all these daffodil bulbs on my kitchen floor for? I don't want them!'

And the gardener said, 'So that's where the daffodils have gone! Wait till I see those dogs!'

Well, he won't see me! I'm under a haystack, fast asleep!

A few daffodils FROM
BOBS 🐾

Dear Children,

I wonder Mistress lets me write to you today, really I do, because Sandy and I are in such disgrace. But it really wasn't our fault – it was all a mistake. You see, we heard Mistress say to Gillian, 'Dilly, let's go and find some old man's beard today. I'd like some for my big blue jar.'

So off they went – and Sandy and I thought we would go and find some too, then Mistress would be very pleased.

Well, no sooner had we got out of the front gate than we saw just what we wanted – a nice old gentleman walking along, with a long grey beard.

'There's old man's beard, Sandy,' I wuffed. 'Come on! We'll get some of it when we've a chance!'

So we followed closely at his heels. He didn't seem to like us at all. He kept shooing us away with his stick, but we always went back.

Then at last he came to a gate and he leaned over it. His

beard fell down the other side, and I said to Sandy, 'Now's our chance!'

So we crept under the gate and I jumped up at the nice old gentleman's beard. He jerked up his head in a fright. Then he saw Mistress and said, 'Madam, will you please call your fierce dogs off! They are attacking me.' Oh, what a story, wasn't it!

'Whatever are you two doing?' Mistress said crossly.

'Only getting some old man's beard for you,' I said. 'We thought you'd be pleased.'

And now it turns out, children, that old man's beard is a fluffy grey plant! Well, who would have thought it?

A FEW WHISKERS FROM
BOBS

Dear Children,

I am getting a bit tired of the trees in our garden. They are so untidy. They keep taking off their leaves and dropping them all over the place. The willow tree over my kennel is the most tiresome of all. It drops leaves on my nose all day long, no matter where I lie. And not only that, the trees and plants are sending off millions of seeds and thistledown comes floating into the garden and settles on my whiskers and makes me sneeze. The pansies wait till I come by, then they explode their seed-boxes and shoot tiny hard seeds all over me! And the sycamore tree sends me presents of seeds with wings that lie about my yard and rustle like mice. I keep popping out to see if a mouse is nibbling my biscuits – but it's only the seeds flying about.

The starlings come into the elderberry tree near by and feast on the purple berries there, dropping purple juice over my nice green kennel. Really, they have dreadful manners, those birds! When I complained about it to Mistress she laughed and said, 'My dear Bobs, the plants have to find *some* way of sending off their seeds! Be careful they don't make *you* help them!'

Oho! *I'm* not helping any plant to send away its seeds – no – I scrape off all those nasty little burr-things that stick to my legs in the field, and bury them deep in the ground. That will get rid of *those*! Don't you think that's clever of me, children?

HiPS aNd hee-haws fROM
BOBS

PS Mistress says it's not clever at all!

Dear Children,

I have written this poem for you. Do you like it?

FIREWORKS

Firework night! You love it, I know,
But oh, boys and girls, I do hate it so!
Those bangs – those fizzes – those great big POPS
And that horrible squib-thing that hisses and hops!
My Mistress is kind – she takes us indoors
Out of the way of the bangs and the roars.
We hide by her knee, and the cats come too,
And we shiver and shake the whole evening through.
But we're glad as can be that we're safely inside
And, please, will you let your pets come in and hide ?
Oh do, boys and girls – you love me, I know,

And this is a way you can easily show
That you are my friends – have I said enough?
I'll just end my thanks to you –
Wuff-wuff-WUFF!

FROM YOUR doggy FRIEND
BOBS

Dear Children,

Did you know that we have had the floods in the fields round about Old Thatch? All my favourite walks have turned into swims. It is such a nuisance. You've no idea how difficult it is to smell down a rabbit-hole that is under the water. Mistress says it's not the slightest use trying to look for rabbits if their holes are under water, but those rabbits are such artful creatures that I wouldn't be a bit surprised to find them in bathing costumes, having a lovely time down their burrows. But when I try to swim under the water to their holes I always seem to float up to the top again. I can't keep down. Sandy says I'm not heavy enough, and he said if I ate half a dozen large stones the weight of them would keep me down nicely. But I can't somehow make up my mind to do that.

Do you know, there is a cheeky little tit that comes to peck at the bone in my yard? It flies off every time I rush at it – but it always comes back again. So this morning I lay down and thought I would pretend to be asleep. Then when the tit came I could snap at it nicely. So down I lay and shut my eyes – and, bones and biscuits, if that cheeky bird didn't fly down to my nose and eat a crumb off my left whiskers! Really, people have no manners at all, these days!

A WHISKERY CRUMB FROM
BOBS

Dear Children,

The other day I found four snails under a stone.

Aha! I thought, *the gardener will perhaps give me a bone for finding these. He doesn't like snails; he says they eat his plants.*

So I went to find the gardener. But I couldn't see him anywhere.

'Look,' said Sandy, 'here's his hat on the ground. Put the snails in there for him to find. He will be so pleased.'

So I dropped the snails in – and then, oh dear, I forgot all about them, and when the gardener did come along at last, he picked up his hat without looking inside and put it on. And all the snails rattled down on to his head.

He was very angry with me, and instead of giving me a bone he chased me all over the garden, and I heard him telling Mistress I was a very naughty dog.

Well, that's the last time I find snails for *him*! Sandy thinks it's very funny, but I don't.

A SNail and a half FROM BOBS

Dear Children,

When I was lying half-asleep in my kennel this morning I heard one of the ducks sneeze. So I looked out to see which one it was – and, oh my goodness, it had sneezed its white feathers off, for they were flying all around in the air as thick as could be!

'Come quick!' I said to Sandy.

So down the garden we ran – and you should have *seen* the feathers! They were flying everywhere, soft white things that didn't make any noise at all! I'd no idea a duck had so many feathers, it was most surprising.

'I do hope we don't sneeze our fur off,' I said to Sandy. 'We *should* look funny.'

Well, we found Mistress, and we told her but, dear me, whatever do you think? Mistress laughed and said, 'Don't be silly, you two dogs! Haven't you ever seen *snow* before!'

But, you know, I still think it *might* have been feathers,

because I did hear that duck sneeze. So now we are going to try and find a duck without any feathers at all, and then we shall take her to Mistress and say, 'We told you so, dear Mistress!'

We're just off to look, so goodbye.

A FEW FEATHERS FROM
BOBS

9th December

Dear Children,

Aren't the nights cold now? Sandy and I cuddle down together in our kennel and keep each other warm, and yesterday the gardener gave us lots more straw to make us cosy.

I heard Mistress say that it was Jack Frost who came at nights and brought the cold weather, and I thought, *Ho! What a miserable rascal he must be! I'll keep a look-out for him and tell him what I think of him!*

So last night Sandy and I kept running out of our kennel trying to spy Jack Frost. Sandy saw the moon, and he thought that was Jack Frost looking down at him through the trees.

My goodness, didn't he bark! Then I thought I heard him pattering along, but it was only the leaves blowing in the wind.

At last we fell asleep – and, will you believe it, in the morning we found he had been! The bold fellow had actually painted our kennel with bits of frost! Tonight I am going to BITE him!

A FROSTY wag FROM BOBS

Dear Children,

Gillian is decorating her nursery for Christmas with bright-coloured paper and streamers, so Sandy and I thought we would decorate our kennel too. We only had straw to do it with and a few old bones, but we have made it quite nice. The straw is all on the roof and so are the bones.

I wish we had a few balloons – but Sandy and I are a bit afraid of them. You know, they haven't very good manners always, and sometimes they give a great cough that sounds like POPPPP! and disappear. That frightens me, because I do hate things that go POP.

Once I accidentally sat down on a big red balloon and you should have heard the POP it gave. It nearly blew me up to the ceiling, and I trembled so much afterwards that Mistress said I made the floor shake. I don't much like Christmas crackers, either – they go BANG when you as much as sniff at them.

Now I'm going Christmas shopping. My purse is hung round my neck. Gillian is going to help me, because she is quite good at shopping now. She lent me the purse. I was going to carry all my pennies in my mouth, but Gillian says they might slip down my throat and then I should rattle like a money-box! Sandy says he'd like to hear me, but I'm not going to let him!

CHRISTMASSY wags, licks, barks
and nibbles from
BOBS

Dear Children,

Well, Christmas is coming again. I've been waiting for it quite a long time now, so I hope it won't take the wrong turning and get lost. Green Hedges is quite difficult to find down our way. Isn't it a pity!

Do you hang up your stockings at Christmas time? Gillian does, and so does Imogen, and they get them full of all sorts of lovely things. The only thing that Sandy and I can hang up is our collars – and they don't hold much. So we've decided to wear stockings and then we can hang them up on Christmas night.

'Where can we get them from?' Sandy said. 'Do they grow anywhere?'

I said, 'Yes, Sandy! I've seen them growing on the clothes-line in the garden! We'll get some from there.'

So we waited till this morning, and then we saw some socks growing on the line. We jumped up and got four in our mouths – two for Sandy and two for me. But they were difficult to get on! Sandy put one on his tail, because he said it went on easily there – but when he wagged his tail the sock flew off! So that wasn't any good.

Well, I'd just managed to get one nicely on my hind foot when Mistress came along – and tails and whiskers, she wasn't a bit pleased! I hid in my kennel – and I'm afraid we won't have any socks or stockings to hang up after all!

Isn't it a pity!

A CHRISTMAS STOCKING FROM BOBS

Dear Children,

Did you have a good Christmas ? I did! So did Sandy and all the other pets. You should have seen the Christmas bone I had – goodness, it must have come from an elephant or a dragon, or some enormous creature, it was so big! It will last me a long time – till next Christmas, I expect. That is, if Sandy will leave it alone.

He is so annoying. When I nibble one end of the bone, he goes to the other end and begins to gnaw *that*! Then I tug, and he tugs, and first he pulls *me* out of the kennel, and then I pull him *into* the kennel, and we growl hard.

Pat came and watched us, and she said, 'Don't talk with your mouth full, you dogs! Don't you know your manners?'

That made me angry, and I ran at her and chased her round the garden.

And will you believe it, when I came back, Sandy had gnawed the knob off *my* end of the bone!

Well, Christmas is gone. I don't know where it's gone, and I wish I did. I wouldn't mind living with it all the year round. Would you? I could easily be on my best behaviour if I did.

SOME VERY good behaviour FROM BOBS

PS My New Year resolution is to try and eat our dinner faster, so that Sandy doesn't get too fat.

Enid Blyton (1897-1968) longed for a pet as a child but was never allowed one. In 1926, now an adult, she welcomed Bobs the fox terrier into her household as her very first pet. From the arrival of Bobs onwards, Enid Blyton's beloved domestic animals featured heavily in her writing.

Letters 'from Bobs' were published weekly in *Teachers World* from 1929–1945, and the comic strip 'Bobs and his Friends' was written by Enid Blyton for *Sunny Stories* magazine between 1937 and 1939. In 1933, Enid Blyton privately published a collection of the letters, titled *Letters from Bobs*, which sold over 10,000 copies in the first six days. Two further collections, published in 1937 and 1938, sold at the same rate.

When the little dog died of old age in 1935, Enid Blyton couldn't bear to acknowledge his death and asked that his grave in her garden be left unmarked. She continued to write weekly letters from Bobs to her young readers for ten years after he had passed away.

Also available:

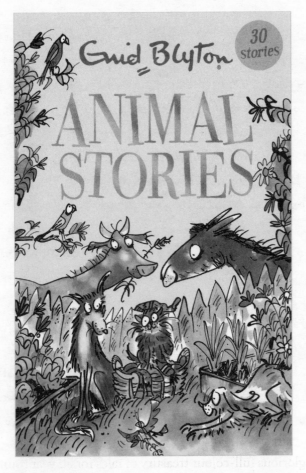

Delve into the world of our furry and feathered friends with these short stories by the world's best-loved storyteller!

Also available:

Enid Blyton

Stories for every Season

Illustrated by Becky Cameron

A glorious full-colour treasury of tales for all year round